PUFFIN BOOKS

The GOLDEN GOOSE

Dick King-Smith served in the Grenadier Guards during the Second World War, and afterwards spent twenty years as a farmer in Gloucestershire, the county of his birth. Many of his stories are inspired by his farming experiences. Later he taught at a village primary school. His first book, *The Fox Busters*, was published in 1978. Since then he has written a great number of children's books, including *The Sheep-Pig* (winner of the Guardian Award and filmed as *Babe*), *Harry's Mad*, *Noah's Brother*, *The Hodgeheg*, *Martin's Mice*, *Ace*, *The Cuckoo Child* and *Harriet's Hare* (winner of the Children's Book Award in 1995). At the British Book Awards in 1991 he was voted Children's Author of the Year. He has three children, a large number of grandchildren and several great-grandchildren, and lives in a seventeenth-century cottage only a crow's-flight from the house where he was born.

Dick King-Smith

The
GOLDEN GOOSE

Illustrated by Ann Kronheimer

PUFFIN

PUFFIN BOOKS

Published by the Penguin Group
Penguin Books Ltd, 80 Strand, London WC2R ORL, England
Penguin Group (USA) Inc., 375 Hudson Street, New York, New York 10014, USA
Penguin Group (Canada), 90 Eglinton Avenue East, Suite 700, Toronto, Ontario, Canada M4P 2Y3
(a division of Pearson Penguin Canada Inc.)
Penguin Ireland, 25 St Stephen's Green, Dublin 2, Ireland (a division of Penguin Books Ltd)
Penguin Group (Australia), 250 Camberwell Road, Camberwell, Victoria 3124, Australia
(a division of Pearson Australia Group Pty Ltd)
Penguin Books India Pvt Ltd, 11 Community Centre, Panchsheel Park, New Delhi – 110 017, India
Penguin Group (NZ), 67 Apollo Drive, Rosedale, North Shore 0632, New Zealand
(a division of Pearson New Zealand Ltd)
Penguin Books (South Africa) (Pty) Ltd, 24 Sturdee Avenue, Rosebank, Johannesburg 2196, South Africa

Penguin Books Ltd, Registered Offices: 80 Strand, London WC2R ORL, England

puffinbooks.com

First published 2003
This edition published 2010
2

Text copyright © Fox Busters Ltd, 2003
Illustrations copyright © Ann Kronheimer, 2003
Extract from *The Schoolmouse:* text copyright © Fox Busters Ltd, 1994
illustrations copyright © Ann Kronheimer, 2003
All rights reserved

The moral right of the author and illustrator has been asserted

Set in 15/18.5pt Perpetua
Made and printed in England by Clays Ltd, St Ives plc

British Library Cataloguing in Publication Data
A CIP catalogue record for this book is available from the British Library

ISBN: 978-0-141-33236-9

www.greenpenguin.co.uk

Mixed Sources
Product group from well-managed
forests and other controlled sources
www.fsc.org Cert no. SA-COC-1592
© 1996 Forest Stewardship Council

Penguin Books is committed to a sustainable future
for our business, our readers and our planet.
The book in your hands is made from paper
certified by the Forest Stewardship Council.

Chapter One

Farmer Skint was a poor unfortunate man.

He was poor because he was not a very good farmer. He always sold things for less than other people did, and he always paid more than other people for whatever he bought.

He was unfortunate because nothing

ever seemed to go right for him. At
haymaking or at
harvest time, it always
seemed to rain. His
cows often got foul-in-
the-foot, his pigs often
got swine fever, and his chickens were
always being eaten by foxes.

There came a time when Farmer Skint
had lost nearly all his animals. He'd had
to sell his remaining cows and pigs and
what chickens were left,
and all he had now on
Woebegone Farm was a

pair of geese: a gander called Misery and a
goose called Sorrow.

'I'm sorry, Janet,' he said to his wife,
'but things have got so bad that we shall
have to sell the farm.'

'Oh no, John, no, John, no!' cried Mrs
Skint. 'What shall we do then? The
children have to be fed and clothed.'

Farmer Skint looked sadly at his two
children, a little girl named
Jill and a baby boy named
Jack. Both looked very
hungry. 'I don't know
about clothes,'

said the farmer, 'but at least we've still got something left to eat.'

'What?' asked Mrs Skint.

'The geese.'

'Oh no, John! Not poor Misery and Sorrow!'

'Well, Misery anyway,' said Farmer Skint. 'Not Sorrow. Not yet. She's sitting on a clutch of eggs. I'll have to let her hatch them out first.'

Later that day he went into his orchard where there was an old hut. Inside it, Sorrow was sitting on her eggs. Misery the gander was standing guard outside and he cackled angrily at the farmer.

'Sorry, old chap,' said Farmer Skint, 'but you may be for the chop one of these fine days.'

Then he went into the hut and carefully
lifted Sorrow off her eggs. She pecked at
him furiously but he was so low-spirited
that he took no notice.

But he took notice quickly enough when
he peeped in the nest.

He'd had a look the day before and there

had been four eggs, four dirty-white
goose eggs, and he was expecting to see
a fifth. He was right. There were now
five eggs.

But what made Farmer Skint gasp with
surprise, what made his heart race and his
breath come quickly, what made his eyes
nearly pop out of his head, was the colour
of that fifth egg. Dirty-
white it was not.
It was golden.

In the weeks that followed, Sorrow sat steadily upon her five eggs, while Misery mounted guard outside the hut. At nights, Farmer Skint shut him inside for fear of the fox.

Then there came a morning when the farmer went into his orchard and was about to open the door of the old hut to let Misery out. But then he thought that the time had come to sacrifice the gander. 'At least,' he said to himself, 'we can have one really good square meal before we all starve,' and he made ready to catch up the bird as he undid the bolt on the door.

Yet it was not Misery who came out first, but Sorrow, and behind her came five newly hatched goslings, and behind them marched their proud father.

Out of the darkness of the hut into the brightness of a lovely May morning they all came, and what he now saw made Farmer Skint catch his breath.

Four of the downy goslings were a pale yellowish colour, like most goslings are, but the fifth one was a wonderful bright gold, all over. Even its beak was gold, as were its little webbed feet.

Out of the golden egg, thought Farmer Skint dazedly, has come a golden gosling that will grow into a golden goose!

As the geese stood around him, waiting for the food in the bucket that the farmer was carrying, the golden gosling waddled right up to his feet and stood looking at him with eyes that were not only bright with intelligence but also golden in colour.

Something made poor unfortunate
Farmer Skint squat down on his heels and
put out a hand and stroke the gosling's
golden back. Had he tried to do this to its
brothers or sisters, they would surely have
backed away, but the golden gosling stood
quite still and even nodded its little head
as though it was enjoying his touch.

But more than that, much more than
that, as he stroked,
Farmer Skint began
gradually to feel
happier. He looked
at his little family
of geese and
knew,

with certainty, that even to feed his own family he could not possibly kill Misery. It was his own misery, he felt, that had suddenly received its death blow.

He looked around his orchard and at his fields beyond and decided he could not possibly sell them. He looked up into the sky and saw what a glorious morning it was, with a sun as golden as his gosling.

Quickly he tipped the food for the geese out of the bucket and ran back to the farmhouse, calling for his wife. When she came out, carrying baby Jack and holding Jill by the hand, she wore a worried face.

'Oh, what is it now, John?' she cried. 'What has happened? What has gone wrong?'

'It's Sorrow,' he said.

'Oh no, John! Not more bad news?'

But then Mrs Skint looked more carefully at her husband and saw that he was smiling. It's ages since I saw him smile, she thought. For that matter, it's ages since I did.

'Come along with me, Janet,' said Farmer Skint, and he led the way out into the orchard, where Misery and Sorrow were finishing their breakfast while their five children pottered about in the sunshine.

'Now then,' said the smiling farmer to his worried wife, 'what d'you think of that, eh?' and he pointed to the golden gosling. 'Just look at the colour of it!'

Mrs Skint looked in wonder, and then, letting go of Jill's hand and holding Jack in

her other arm, she bent down and stroked
that downy golden back. As
she did so, the look of
worry gradually left
her face and she too
began to smile.

Husband and wife
looked at one
another.

'D'you feel as
happy as I do?'
asked the
farmer.

'Oh yes, John, yes, John, yes! I felt it the
moment I touched her.'

'Her?'

'Yes. Something tells me it's a little
goose, not a gander.'

'Well, we'd better think of a name for her,' said Farmer Skint. 'She may be the daughter of Misery and Sorrow but she'll have to have a happier name than that.'

'How about Joy?' suggested his wife.

'Joy,' said Farmer Skint. 'That's perfect. Just what we need.'

Chapter Two

As they walked back up to the farmhouse,
they met the postman, who had parked
his van by the garden wall and was just
about to walk up the path to the front
door. Instead, he handed the letters to the
farmer.

'Thank you! Thank you very much!' said
Farmer Skint. 'It's a beautiful morning,

isn't it? Makes you glad to be alive!'

Whatever's come over him? thought the postman as he drove away. Usually he's a miserable sort of fellow. In fact, I've never seen him smile before, but just now he was grinning like a Cheshire cat.

Farmer Skint ate his breakfast, the letters lying unopened on the table beside him. It was his habit not to look at anything the postman might have brought until he'd finished eating. By then he'd feel more able to deal with the post, which consisted mostly of bills.

'A good dish of bacon and eggs for breakfast,' Farmer Skint's father had been used to say, 'and a man can face up to anything. Bacon and eggs give a good lining to the stomach.'

But now there were no pigs or chickens on Woebegone Farm, so the poor unfortunate farmer had to make do with toast and a scrape of jam. Unfortunate he may have been, and poor, at that moment, he still was, yet he ate his food with gusto. Then he took a paper-knife and slit open the three envelopes which the postman had brought.

The first two contained bills and for a moment his smiles were replaced by a frown, but then he opened the third envelope and the frown vanished, to be replaced by a look of total amazement.

After a while he raised his head and looked around the kitchen table, at baby Jack in his high chair, at little Jill, at his wife.

'Would you be*lieve* it!' said Farmer Skint in a hoarse whisper.

'Believe what, John?' asked Mrs Skint, her smiles now changing to a frown.

'I've been and gone and won the

Premium Bonds, that's all,' said her husband.

'What d'you mean?'

'Well, years and years ago, when I was a boy, my old dad bought me a Premium Bond. A one-pound bond it was. It never won anything of course. Till now.'

Farmer Skint looked at his wife and his face broke into the biggest smile you can imagine.

'Till now,' he said again. 'Now it has won something, Janet, that old one-pound bond has. Guess how much.'

'Oh, I don't know, John,' said Mrs Skint. 'Ten pounds perhaps?'

'A lot more than that.'

'A hundred pounds?'

'Not enough noughts.'

'Oh no, John, don't tell me – you've never won a thousand pounds, have you?'

'No,' said Farmer Skint. 'This letter is to say that that old Premium Bond that my old dad bought me has won ten thousand pounds! Look, here's the cheque,' and he waved it in front of his wife.

Pay John Skint £10,000

'Oh John!' gasped Mrs Skint in a choked voice. 'Our luck has changed at last.'

'Looks like it,' said the farmer. 'We shall have money in the bank again. Or we shall have once I've paid this cheque in. There's still a drop of petrol left in the old car, so leave the washing-up – we'll all go straight into town.'

'And buy some new clothes for the children,' Mrs Skint said.

'And food, all sorts of food, specially bacon and eggs. We'll have a second breakfast when we get back.'

'And we'll get sweets for the children.'

'And petrol for the car.'

'And new shoes for the children.'

'And, Janet, you could have a new washing machine.'

'And a new fridge.'

'And a new telly.'

'And toys for the children.'

'And it's Market Day tomorrow. I could buy a couple of cows.'

'And some hens.'

'And a pig or two.'

'And perhaps a pet rabbit for the children. Oh John, everything in the garden is lovely, and you know why, don't you?'

'Yes. I've just won ten thousand pounds.'

'Yes, but why have you? What's happened to change you from a poor unfortunate man to a rich and lucky one? Who is the cause of all this luck?'

'It must be Joy,' said Farmer Skint.

Chapter Three

What a shopping spree the Skints had that day! As well as buying some of the things they'd talked about, Farmer Skint bought a big sack of corn for the geese and a few sacks of meal and bran which he would mix together to make their daily mash. Misery and Sorrow had been living on rather poor rations recently and they were

obviously delighted to be given much
more food.

'Kark! Kark!' they cried in their
pleasure.

But one morning, after the farmer had
given them their breakfast and was eating
his own (a good dish of bacon and eggs),
he suddenly heard them making quite a
different noise – a loud, urgent honking
which meant, he knew, that were was
danger about. Geese are good watchdogs,

which is why the ancient Romans kept them to guard their most important temple. They knew the geese would make a great din if enemies approached.

Farmer Skint was neither ancient nor a Roman, but as soon as he heard the row that Misery and Sorrow were making, he jumped up from the breakfast table. On his way out of the farmhouse, he grabbed his gun, for he had a pretty good idea of what the approaching enemy was.

He was right. Sneaking among the orchard trees was a red bushy-tailed figure.

Misery and Sorrow stood bravely side by side facing the fox, their children grouped behind them. Farmer Skint ducked down behind the low wall of the orchard. His

two geese
would, he knew,
do their best to
protect their
family, even at
the cost of their
own lives, but the
goslings would be
easy meat for the red
raider, who was by
now very close.

Long muzzle pointed
ahead, eyes fixed upon its
intended prey, the fox was poised for a

final deadly rush, when Farmer Skint fired both barrels.

The alarm cries of the geese now changed to shouts of triumph as the farmer came forward to pick up the limp body of their enemy.

'And d'you know what, Janet?' he said to his wife later. 'Misery and Sorrow and four of the goslings just went off down to the pond as though nothing had happened. But the golden one –'

'Joy,' said Mrs Skint.

'Yes, Joy – she stood looking at that old

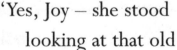

dead fox and then she looked up at me,
and it seemed almost as though . . .'

'What?' asked Mrs Skint.

'As though she was saying thank you.'

'Well, you saved her life.'

'Thank goodness,' said Farmer Skint.
'I couldn't bear to lose her.'

'I suppose we could shut them all up in
the daytime,' said Mrs Skint.

'Shut them up? Where?'

'Well, in the empty cowshed. Then, if
another fox comes, they'd be safe.'

'But the old ones would be miserable,
Janet. You know how they like grazing the
orchard grass and swimming in the pond.
We'll just have to be on the look-out from
now on, or rather on the listen-out,
because Misery and Sorrow will give the

alarm if there's any danger in the daytime.
I wouldn't worry all that much if it wasn't
for Joy.'

'Well, put *her* in the cowshed.'

'All on her own? No, no. But I don't
know what to do. It's a problem.'

But that very afternoon the problem was
solved. Farmer Skint had just given the
geese their midday mash and was
standing, watching them eat. He was
thinking, as he so often did, how beautiful
the golden gosling was. She's safe at night,
he thought. If only I could be sure that
she'd be safe by day.

As he walked back up to the farmhouse,
he had a sudden feeling that he was being
followed. He looked round, and there was
Joy, pattering along at his heels. He

stopped. She stopped. He went on again. She came after him.

Reaching the door of the farmhouse, Farmer Skint opened it and, turning, said to Joy, by way of a joke, 'Do come in, won't you?'

She did.

'Oh look, Mummy!' cried little Jill, and she ran forward and began to stroke the gosling's golden back. As she did so, she broke into a huge smile.

Then baby Jack came crawling across the floor and touched Joy. As he did so, he began to chortle with delight.

'Look at them!' said the children's

mother. 'They love her, don't they? I don't know what we'd do without her now.'

'She'd be quite safe in here,' said Farmer Skint.

'In here, John?' asked his wife. 'Whatever do you mean? You're surely not thinking of having her live in the house? Only dogs and cats live in people's houses. She's a goose. Just think of the messes she'd make.'

'I could house-train her, Janet,' said Farmer Skint.

'What, to go outside to do her business, like you'd teach a puppy to do?'

'Yes, or better still, we could give her a litter tray, like you would for a kitten. I bet she'd soon learn to use it. Come to think of it, there's an old plastic seed tray in the greenhouse that would do fine. I'll get it now,' said the farmer, and he went out. Joy followed him. Before long he came back with the seed tray, in which he'd put a layer of peat. Joy was still following him.

He placed the tray in a corner of the room.

'Now then,' he said to the golden gosling, 'if you want to do something, you do it in there, OK?'

Mrs Skint laughed. 'Don't be silly, John,' she said. 'How could the poor little thing possibly understand what you're saying?'

Hardly were the words out of her mouth when Joy waddled over to the seed tray, climbed into it and did a poo. Somehow neither of the Skints was all that surprised

to see that, instead of the usual dirty-
white colour that birds' droppings are,
these were golden.

'Clever girl!' said Farmer Skint to his gosling, and to his wife, 'I bet you she would, didn't I?'

He sat down and looked at his watch. 'It would have been time for afternoon milking now,' he said, 'after I'd fed the pigs and the chickens. But now there are no animals left, so there's no hurry to do anything. I could get used to a life like this, Janet.'

'That Premium Bond money's not going to last us forever, you know,' his wife said.

'You're right,' said her husband. 'But then, you never know, Joy might bring us another bit of luck. So shall I put the kettle on? We'll have a cup of tea while I have a look at today's paper.'

While Farmer Skint was sitting at the

kitchen table, Joy was standing beside his chair, looking up at him.

'She's certainly taken a fancy to you, John,' said Mrs Skint.

The farmer put down a hand and stroked the gosling. Then he opened his newspaper. By chance it fell open at the sports pages, and by chance his gaze fell upon the runners and riders for the afternoon's racing at Ascot.

'Well, would you believe it!' he cried loudly.

'What?' asked Mrs Skint.

'Look here! Just look at this! I'm not a gambling man, Janet, you know that, but don't you think I ought to have a bet on this one? It's running in the four-thirty — I've just got time to get some money on it,' and he pointed at the name of one particular horse.

Chapter Four

'Goodness!' said Mrs Skint. 'You'll have to have a flutter on that, John, won't you!'

Farmer Skint looked at his watch again.

'I'd better get down to the betting shop straight away,' he said.

'But John, your tea?'

'When I get back. It's ten past four

already. I've got to get there before the race starts. I must find my wallet.'

Farmer Skint had never been inside a betting shop before and didn't know quite what to do. He went to the counter and said, 'Excuse me, I want to put some money on a horse.'

The clerk handed him a slip.

'Fill in the horse's name,' he said, 'and the name of the meeting and the time of the race and the amount of your stake.'

'Stake?' said Farmer Skint.

'How much money you're going to bet.'

How much money am I going to bet? the farmer asked himself. He took out his wallet, bulging these days thanks to the Premium Bond win. Then he filled in the betting slip.

BETS

JOHN'S JOY. Ascot. 4.30. £10.

He took a ten-pound note from the
wallet.

'Better hurry, sir,' said the clerk.
'They're going down to the start now.'

But then Farmer Skint suddenly
thought, If I'm going to have a gamble, I'll
have a real gamble. After all, I'm backing
the golden gosling, aren't I? She'll make it
come right. He took nine more notes
from the wallet and altered the ten
pounds to a hundred pounds. The clerk
took the betting slip and the money
without saying anything, but he couldn't

help raising his eyebrows. Whatever's this
country bumpkin up to? he thought.
Never had a bet in his life before by the
look of him, and now he's going to chuck
away a hundred quid on a horse that
hasn't got a hope of winning. He looked at
the starting prices:

JOHN'S JOY 50–1.

He looked at Farmer Skint and he shook his head sadly.

'They'll be off in a minute, sir,' he said, 'if you'd care to watch.'

'Watch?' said the farmer.

The clerk pointed to the rows of television screens on the walls of the betting shop.

Farmer Skint watched open-mouthed as the runners in the four-thirty at Ascot burst from their starting stalls.

'The early leader,' came the voice of the commentator, 'is Sweet Thursday by a couple of lengths from Guardian Angel in second, followed by Merry Music. The

rest are fairly tightly bunched, with the
exception of John's Joy, who is bringing
up the rear.'

Farmer Skint watched the galloping
horses, not knowing the number or the
colours of John's Joy, let alone the odds
against it winning. But he could see that
there was one horse behind all the others.
Before he could begin to worry, he heard
the commentator saying, 'They're coming
to the halfway mark now and Sweet
Thursday's dropping back. Merry Music
takes up the running by a length from
Guardian Angel, and the rest are getting a
bit strung out as the leader passes the
three-furlong post. The early front-
runner, Sweet Thursday, has faded and
John's Joy is beginning to make good

progress through the field. In fact, as they reach the two-furlong post John's Joy is only a couple of lengths off the lead and going well. Will there be an upset here, I wonder? Is the outsider going to get into the frame? John's Joy is on Merry Music's shoulder now at the furlong post – now they're neck and neck – fifty yards to go – it's John's Joy! John's Joy's the winner! It's John's Joy by a length – the outsider's beaten the lot of them!'

She did it! Farmer Skint said to himself. Joy did it! and he went to the counter and handed over his betting slip.

'My horse won,' he said. 'How much do I get?'

'The starting price,' said the clerk in a strained voice, 'was fifty to one.'

'I'm no good at arithmetic,' said Farmer Skint.

'You've won five thousand pounds, sir,' said the clerk, and he began counting from a wad of fifty-pound notes.

'. . . A hundred . . . a hundred and one . . . a hundred and two,' he finished, and handed over the thick packet of notes.

'Wait a minute,' said Farmer Skint. 'You said I'd won five thousand pounds but you've given me a hundred and two fifty-pound notes. That makes five thousand, one hundred. You've given me too much.'

The clerk sighed.

'No, sir,' he said. 'Your stake was a
hundred pounds – that's what you bet –
so, because you won, you get that back.
Five thousand pounds plus one hundred
equals five thousand, one hundred.'

'So it does,' said Farmer Skint. 'I'm

much obliged,' and out of the betting shop he went.

Country bumpkin my foot! thought the clerk. He knew what he was doing all right.

Farmer Skint did not go straight back to Woebegone Farm. He went first to a wine merchant's, then to a toyshop, and then to a jeweller's. As nearly as he could (for he was not good at arithmetic), he spent the hundred pounds that he had staked on a horse —

and very much enjoyed doing so.

When he came into the farmhouse, laden with parcels, his wife took one look at them and cried, 'Oh John, you must have won!'

'I did,' said her husband, 'or rather John's Joy did. So I've bought you all presents.'

He put the parcels down on the kitchen table and said to his little daughter, 'This is for you, Jill.' It was a beautiful doll.

Then he said to his baby son, 'And this is for you, Jack.' It was a big teddy bear.

And to his wife he said, 'There are lots of good things in small parcels, Janet,' and watched as she undid a very small packet. In it was a pretty necklace.

'Oh John,' she said, 'how lovely! Fancy

buying all these things for us. You must
have won a lot.'

'I did.'

'Well, you'd better have that cup of
tea then.'

'No,' said Farmer
Skint, 'I think we'll
have something
a bit

special,
to celebrate,'
and he unwrapped
a large bottle of
champagne. Mrs Skint
and her children and the
golden gosling all watched
as he eased off the cork, and
all jumped when it came out

with a very loud pop. Then Farmer Skint
poured the golden wine into two glasses.

'Cheers, Janet!' he said.

'Cheers, John!' she replied. 'My
goodness me, you must have won an awful
lot of money to be able to buy all these
presents.'

'I did,' said her husband, and he took
from his wallet that thick wad of
fifty-pound notes and laid
it on the table.

'Count those,'
he said.

Mrs Skint did
so, looking
more and
more amazed.

'There's a

hundred of them!' she said in a dazed
voice.

'Quite right,' said Farmer Skint. 'That's
what I won. Or I suppose I should say,
John's Joy won it,' and he poured a little
champagne into a saucer and set it on the
floor before the golden gosling.

'She won't drink that, John!' laughed
Mrs Skint.

'She will,' said Farmer Skint.

And she did.

Chapter Five

At first Farmer Skint only allowed Joy to
be a house-goose by day. At night he shut
her in the old hut with her family. But one
evening he thought to himself, she's so
good, never makes a mess in the house,
always uses her litter tray, doesn't make a
noise – she's no trouble at all. I'll let her
stay in the kitchen tonight.

After the children had been put to bed
and it was beginning to get dark, Mrs
Skint said, 'Have you shut the geese up,
John?'

'Yes, I have.'

'But you've forgotten Joy.'

'No, I haven't. I thought she could stop
in with us.'

'Oh John, you make a fool of yourself
over that bird!'

'Maybe, Janet, but that bird's made a
new man of me.'

And it was true. Not only was it due to
Joy, Farmer Skint thought, that he had
won on the Premium Bond, and the
horse-race, but also, he thought, she had
somehow changed him from a loser to a
winner.

Before May was
out, he had bought
a bunch of good-
quality heifers, and
a couple of well-bred sows, and a flock of
handsome young
chickens (which he
housed in a fox-
proof enclosure).

He had not paid
more than other
people for this livestock, as he once
would have done, but less. And later in
the year, when he came to sell his eggs
and his piglets and the
occasional bull-
calf, he did not sell
for less than other

people, as he once would have done, but for more.

That bird has made a new man of him indeed! Mrs Skint thought now. And a new woman of me, for that matter, and the children love her. It's almost as though I had another child in the house.

'All right, John,' she said. 'Try keeping her in the kitchen tonight, but mind – any messes, she's out.'

'There won't be any,' said Farmer Skint. And there weren't.

So Joy became a full-time house-goose. To be sure, she saw her parents every day, for she always followed the farmer down to the orchard when he went to feed them (he'd sold the other four goslings — for a handsome price, what's more), and Misery and Sorrow were always noisily pleased to see this golden child of theirs.

But Farmer Skint was careful not to take Joy outside unless he was sure there was nobody about. As things were now, he no longer worried too much about foxes, but human thieves would be a different matter. If a dishonest person were to set eyes on his extraordinary bird, she might be stolen.

Really, the only person likely to see Joy was the postman. Nobody else much ever

came to the Skints' isolated farmhouse.
When the new flock of chickens began to
lay, Mrs Skint took the eggs she had for
sale to the market in town. She didn't
want people knocking on her door.

The postman didn't usually knock, he
just shoved the mail through the flap of
the letter box in the front door – unless
he had a parcel too big to go through the
flap, in which case he'd press the bell.

One morning towards the end of June,
when Farmer Skint was making hay (no
rain about now, the weather was glorious
and stayed so throughout haymaking and,
later, harvest), the postman came to
Woebegone Farm with a biggish parcel
and pressed the bell. Mrs Skint didn't
hear the ring because she was hoovering,

but Jill did and went
to the front door. She
was not tall enough to
open it, but just the right
height for talking through
the flap of the letter box.

'Who is it?' she asked.

'Postman, dear,' said the
postman. 'I've got a parcel
for your mummy.'

'I can't open the door. I'm not tall
enough.'

'Well, don't worry, I'll leave it on the step and you'll tell her, will you?'

'All right,' said Jill.

'Bye-bye then,' said the postman.

'We've got a golden goose,' said Jill.

'You've got a what?'

'A golden goose. She's called Joy.'

'Fancy!' said the postman. Kids! he thought. They say some funny things. And he got in his van and drove away.

Chance plays a great part in the lives of people, and of geese for that matter.

If the postman hadn't had a parcel to deliver, he wouldn't have rung the bell.

If Mrs Skint hadn't been hoovering, she'd have heard it and gone to the door instead of Jill.

If the postman hadn't sounded so nice

through the flap, Jill might not have told him about the golden goose.

But the biggest 'if' was to do with one of the Skints' nearest neighbours. Not that any of them lived very close to Woebegone Farm, but a couple of miles away there was a large country house that was also on the postman's rounds.

It was called Galapagos House, and it belonged to a famous naturalist and broadcaster called Sir David Otterbury.

And the final strange chance that came about that morning was that when the postman arrived at Galapagos House and knocked on its front door (for here too he had a parcel to deliver), the door was opened by Sir David himself.

The postman knew him of course, as did millions of people who had watched his many television programmes about all sorts of animals in all parts of the world, and it struck him that the great man might be amused to be told what the Skints' child had said.

'Good morning, sir. Parcel for you,' he said.

'Thank you,' replied Sir David Otterbury.

'I heard a funny thing this morning, sir,'

said the postman. 'You know all about geese, I'm sure.'

'I know a bit about them.'

'Well, you know the Skints, sir? Woebegone Farm?'

'I don't know them, but I had heard they'd fallen on hard times.'

'Oh, their luck's changed,' said the postman, 'so folk say. But anyway, what I was going to tell you was that I was talking to the Skints' little girl this morning, through their letter flap.'

'Through their letter flap?'

'Yes, she's not tall enough to open the door – and you'll never guess what she said to me. She told me they'd got a golden goose. Funny the things kids say, isn't it?'

'A *golden* goose?' said Sir David Otterbury.

'Don't suppose you've ever heard of such a bird, sir,' said the postman. 'I thought you'd be amused.'

After the postman had driven away, Sir David went to his study to open his parcel and to read the rest of his mail. But all the time, as he was always interested to hear about different beasts and birds, he kept thinking about what the child had said. A golden goose? No such bird, surely.

Yet the phrase rang a bell in his mind. Was it a story he'd heard on his travels? Was it something he'd heard as a child – a fairy story, perhaps? No, don't be so silly, he said to himself. The little girl was talking nonsense or perhaps just talking about one of her toys. Maybe she'd got her birds muddled and it was a golden pheasant that the Skints had. But a golden goose! Rubbish! Still, thought Sir David, I'd quite like to go and have a look and see what bird it is.

Chapter Six

Sir David Otterbury was, of course, a very busy man. He was abroad a good deal, making nature programmes in various parts of the world, and even in England he was often away from Galapagos House on business of one sort or another. So it was in fact many months before he was reminded of the postman's

story of the little girl who said she had a
golden goose.

But then one day he was driving along a
country road not too far from his home
and there was the signpost for
WOEBEGONE FARM. It pointed
up a very narrow lane.
Ah, thought Sir
David, the
golden goose!

I'll have a peep and see if I can spot this ridiculous bird. I'll pretend I've come to buy some hens' eggs. And he turned up the lane.

Nearing the farmhouse, he saw an orchard with an old hut in it and a pond and a pair of geese, grazing side by side.

Ordinary white geese, thought Sir David. No more golden than I am. Why am I wasting my time? I'll turn round and go back.

But just at that moment Farmer Skint came out of the farmhouse and approached the car.

'Looking for me?' he asked, and then he recognized the face of the driver – a face that he had seen so many times on his television set. The driver smiled at him.

'Good afternoon,' he said. 'My name's David Otterbury.'

'Yes, sir, I know,' said the farmer. What's he want? he thought.

'Could you sell me a dozen eggs? I'd be most grateful.'

'Certainly,' replied Farmer Skint. 'I'll fetch them right away.'

Thought for a moment he might have heard about Joy, he said to himself as he went to get a tray of eggs. Don't see how he could have done, though. But then he suddenly thought how interested Sir David Otterbury would be. Of all the people in the land, he'd be the one who'd be the most interested. Shall I let him see her? thought Farmer Skint. But then he'd tell the world about her, wouldn't he? Not if I swore him to secrecy, though – if I made him promise not to tell.

Farmer Skint still hadn't made his mind up what to do when he came back with the tray of eggs.

'Here you are, sir,' he said to Sir David, who had got out of his car and was leaning on the wall of the orchard, looking at Misery and Sorrow.

'Thank you, Mr Skint,' he said.

'You know my name,
Sir David?'

'Yes.'

'Everybody knows yours,' said the
farmer. He looked at that pleasant smiling
face, and made up his mind in a flash.

'You know all about geese, I'm sure,' he said.

'I know a bit about them. You've got a handsome pair out there. Have you bred from them?'

'Yes, sir, I have,' said Farmer Skint. He took a deep breath. 'I'd like to show you what I've bred from them, if you've got a minute.'

'Certainly.'

'There's just one thing, sir. I don't want anyone else to know. Will you promise not to breathe a word of it to anybody else?'

Don't tell me, thought Sir David, that your little daughter was telling the truth to the postman! Golden goose indeed! It'll just be a brownish sort of bird, I expect. But I would like to see it.

'Certainly, Mr Skint,' he said. 'I promise not to tell a soul.'

Farmer Skint went back into the farmhouse and a few minutes later came out again, followed by Joy.

Never, for the rest of his life, did Sir
David Otterbury forget the thrill of
delight he felt at the sight that met his
astonished eyes. For walking sedately at
the heels of Farmer Skint of Woebegone
Farm was a full-grown goose, a goose that
was a wonderful bright gold colour all
over. Even its beak was gold, as were its
large webbed feet, and it stared up at him
with its golden eyes.

'Ever seen one like this before?' said
Farmer Skint.

Sir David Otterbury had, in his time,
met many different sorts of geese. Aside
from ordinary farmyard geese, he had
seen barnacle geese, and Canada geese,
and white-fronted, and pink-footed, and
lots more. But never had he set eyes on

such a goose as this.

'Did I understand you to say, Mr Skint,' he said, 'that you had bred this bird?'

'Yes, sir. From Sorrow and Misery out there in the orchard. Sorrow hatched four normal goslings and this one. Give her a stroke, Sir David. She likes that.'

The naturalist bent down and ran the palm of his hand gently over the

feathers of the golden goose, and as he did so, he began to smile broadly.

'It's a funny thing, Mr Skint,' he said, 'but touching this extraordinary bird of yours has made me feel on top of the world! Do you find she has that effect on you?'

'I do, sir. We all do.'

'What is she called?'

'Joy.'

'That,' said Sir David, 'is exactly what I feel.'

Chapter Seven

In the weeks that followed, life went on
very pleasantly at Woebegone Farm.
Farmer Skint's new dairy cattle milked
well, his sows gave birth to large litters of
piglets and his hens produced masses of
eggs.

However, life at Galapagos House was
less serene. Not that Sir David Otterbury

was unhappy – how could he be when he had touched the golden goose? – but he was in a worried state of mind. It was very hard to know that this wonderful and unique bird was within a few miles of him and not to be able to tell the world about it. But he couldn't say a word – he had promised Farmer Skint that he would not.

Now that he had seen Joy, he began to feel sure that somewhere, in some book or other, at some time or other, he had once read something about a golden goose. It was an old story, he was sure, that he had come across. He searched through the dozens of bird books in the library of Galapagos House but could find nothing.

Then one night he had a strange dream,

and when he woke up he remembered
two strange words from this dream.

Sir David realized, first, that these two words were in Latin and, second, that what they meant in English was

GOOSE OF A GOLDEN COLOUR.

The Romans! he thought excitedly. That was it, that was what I came across once! The Romans had something to do with a golden goose. And he bolted his breakfast and jumped in his car and raced off to the nearest large public library.

After a great deal of searching through books on Roman stories and legends, he found what he had been looking for.

The Legend of the Golden Goose

*During the reign of the Emperor Nero
(AD 37–68) there began a belief that one day
there would be hatched, from a golden egg, a
golden gosling that would grow into a golden
goose. This bird would be possessed of magical
powers, which would bring happiness,
contentment and good fortune to anyone who
touched it. As it grew older, however, the bird,
though keeping its magic gifts, would gradually
lose its distinctive colour. Eventually it would
look exactly like an ordinary farmyard goose. At
no time during the period of the Roman
Empire (27 BC–AD 476) was there ever any
report of such a bird, and therefore the legend
of the golden goose was gradually forgotten.*

'But not by me!' said Sir David to himself. 'Those old Romans were right – Joy does have magic powers, I'm sure. But what if they were also right about her losing her colour? Somehow I must try to persuade Farmer Skint to release me from my promise, to allow me to show his wonderful bird on television before she becomes as ordinary to look at as Misery and Sorrow. What if she's already begun to change colour?'

Hastily he jumped in his car again and whizzed off to

Woebegone Farm. He found the farmer
mucking out his cowshed.

'Good morning, Mr Skint,' he said.

'John's the name, Sir David,' replied
Farmer Skint.

'Right,' said the great naturalist. 'John it is, and you can drop the "Sir". I get enough of that. Now then, tell me, how is Joy?'

'She's fine, sir,' said Farmer Skint.

Sir David Otterbury held up a finger. 'Now, now,' he said, 'what was I just saying?'

'Oh, sorry, er, David,' said the farmer. 'She's fine.'

'Still that glorious golden colour all over, eh?'

'Oh yes. Though there is one funny thing I noticed. Only this morning I saw it.'

'Saw what?'

'Well,' said John Skint, 'I told you, didn't I, that Joy is house-trained? She does her business in a litter tray, like a cat would. But I don't think I told you that her droppings are always gold-coloured too. And this morning they weren't. They were just dirty-white, like her mum's and her dad's.'

Oh, misery and sorrow! thought Sir David. It's started!

Chapter Eight

It's now or never, said Sir David to himself, and to Farmer Skint he said, 'John, my friend, will you do me a great favour?'

'Of course, sir – I mean, of course, David,' replied the farmer. 'What is it?'

'Will you release me from my promise to you to say nothing about Joy? Will you allow me to tell two other people – two people I have worked with for many years and would trust to keep the secret of your golden goose?'

'Who are these two people?' John Skint asked.

'One is a cameraman, the other a sound recordist. If you will allow me, I will arrange for them to come here, to Woebegone Farm, and film Joy as soon as possible.'

'For the television?'

'Yes.'

'But that's the last thing I want,' said Farmer Skint. 'Why, if you showed her on the telly I'd have the whole world knocking on my door. We'd never have any peace – and what's more, there'd be

lots of people wanting to see her, touch
her, steal her even. No, no, David, you
can't do that to me, not after you
promised.'

'Hang on a minute, John,' said Sir David
Otterbury. 'There's something you don't
know about. Hear me out while I make
you another promise, which is – I will not
show any film of your golden goose as
long as she is still golden.'

'Whatever do you mean? She always
will be.'

'She may not,' said Sir David, and he
told the farmer about the Roman legend.

'She may change, you see,' he said.
'Today her droppings are no longer gold.
Tomorrow – next week, next month, who
knows – it may be her feet or her beak or

her eyes that lose their colour, and then
her feathers, until she is a golden goose
no longer. But John, if only you will allow
me to film her now, then we will have a
record of her for all time. I promise not
to show the film on television till she's
lost all her colour.'

'And if she doesn't?'

'Then I won't show it at all. I'll keep it
as a private record of her, just for your
family and for me.'

Suppose those old Romans were right?
Farmer Skint thought. Suppose that
before long Joy will be golden no more? It
would be dreadful not to have a picture of
his beautiful golden goose.

'All right, David,' he said at last. 'You go
ahead. I trust you.'

'Thank you, John,' said Sir David Otterbury. 'And just remember that if a film of Joy is ever shown on television, they'll pay a great deal of money for it and I'll make sure that a large part of it comes to you.'

Sir David worked fast. Two days later he was out in the orchard at Woebegone Farm with his cameraman and sound recordist, giving a commentary as Joy walked down to the pond between her proud white parents, and the three of them swam together in the morning sunshine.

'Never,' he said, 'has such a bird as this been seen before. Golden from top to toe – feathers, eyes, beak, feet – this goose is a creature hitherto unknown to science,

and is certainly the most amazing discovery of my life as a naturalist. The only reference to it was made by the ancient Romans nearly two thousand years ago, some of whom believed in the magic powers of the bird they called "Anser Aureus", the Golden Goose. To touch it, they said, was to experience instant happiness.'

No sooner had he finished speaking into the microphone than Joy left Misery and Sorrow floating on the sunlit water. She walked up out of the pond

and waddled straight towards the camera
and stopped and stood, waiting. And Sir
David Otterbury stepped into shot and
bent and stroked her golden back.

Then he straightened up and turned to
the camera, his face wreathed in smiles.

'The Romans were
right!' he said.

Chapter Nine

As they drove away from Woebegone
Farm, the cameraman said to the sound
recordist, 'What a bird, eh?'

'Never seen anything like it,' replied the
other, 'and nor has the old Otter either.
Never seen him so pleased. I mean, when
we were filming those mountain gorillas,
years ago, remember? And they were

crawling all over him and he was looking as though he loved it? But today he looked even happier.'

'Yes,' agreed the cameraman. 'I got some lovely shots.'

'And I got some good wild track too,' said the sound recordist. 'Cows mooing, birds singing, and those two old white geese honking away – to show how proud they were of their daughter, I suppose.'

'Someone's going to pay a great deal of money to show this little bit of film we've just made.'

'Not half! Pity it has to be a secret,' said the sound recordist, 'but when the old Otter tells me to keep shtoom, I keep shtoom.'

Sir David Otterbury, meanwhile, had gone back to Galapagos House. Before he left, he said to Farmer Skint, 'Now, John, as soon as that bit of film is processed and edited, you must all come over to my place and see it.'

'See it? On the telly, you mean? But you promised you wouldn't show it while she's still golden!'

'No, not on the telly. I've got my own

little projection room at Galapagos House
— a kind of mini-cinema. I'll show you the
film there when it's ready. Now please
will you promise me something, John,
before I go?'

'What?'

'Promise to let me know when there's
any further loss of colour from your
wonderful golden goose.'

'You think there's bound to be, do you,
David?'

'I've a nasty feeling that those old
Romans were right. But try not to worry
too much, John. They also said that such a
bird would still retain its magic gifts.'

A week later the phone rang in
Galapagos House.

'Hullo, David Otterbury here.'

'It's John Skint.'

'John, what news?'

'The Romans were right. The colour has nearly gone from her webs and her beak and her eyes.'

'What about her plumage?'

'Not as bright as it was.'

'Thank goodness I persuaded him to let me make that film!' said Sir David to himself as he put the phone down.

Looks like we were only just in time.

A couple of weeks later two things happened: the film of Joy, the golden goose, arrived at Galapagos House, and at Woebegone Farm Joy was golden no longer.

Sir David came over the next day and they all went out into the orchard together, he and John Skint and Janet Skint and Jill Skint and Jack Skint (who was toddling by now). They stood looking at not two but three ordinary white geese.

'Which is Joy?' asked Jill.

'Joy gone?' asked Jack.

'No,' said Farmer Skint. 'She hasn't gone. She's just changed colour, that's all. She's still our lucky magic goose.' And he called, 'Come, Joy!' and one of the three white geese waddled forward and stood before them, and each of them in turn stroked the feathers of her back, feathers that had been brilliant gold and were now dull white.

But all of them, from the oldest to the youngest, felt a thrill of happiness and contentment as they stroked, and little Jack summed the whole thing up.

'Joy not gone!' he said happily.

That afternoon the Skints all went over to Galapagos House to see the film. The voice-over, the camerawork, the sound

were all perfect, and no one in the world,
seeing the shots of Joy, would ever be able
to doubt that there was such a bird as a
golden goose.

After tea – with hot buttered crumpets for John and Janet and chocolate-chip ice cream for Jill and Jack – Sir David Otterbury said to Farmer Skint, 'Now then, John, what are we going to do? Are we going to keep this film to ourselves, or are we going to show the golden goose to the world?'

John Skint turned to his wife. 'What do you think, Janet?'

'I think,' said Janet Skint, 'that Sir David would be very disappointed if he couldn't show the film on television. And it would be lovely for other people and their children to see our Joy as she used to be. After all, no one can bother us about it – we haven't got a golden goose any more. But just think how interested thousands of

other people would
be to see her.'

'Millions,' said
Sir David. 'And as I
told your
husband, Mrs
Skint, the
television
companies will
fight tooth and nail for the rights
to screen this film. They will pay a great
deal of money for it, I've no doubt, and I
will pay John a very fair share of it.'

That goose, thought Janet Skint – she
doesn't half earn us money, one way or
another.

'I'm happy about it, John,' she said to
her husband, 'if you are.'

'I am,' said
John Skint.
'And so am I,'
said Jill Skint.
As for Jack
Skint, it was
all a bit
confusing
for him,
but he was
very happy because
of what he'd just seen.
'Joy gold again!' he said.

Chapter Ten

When that film of the golden goose was shown on television – not just British television but all over the world – it created an enormous sensation. Sir David Otterbury received a huge amount of praise (and indeed a huge amount of money, a very fair share of which went, as had been promised, into

Farmer Skint's pockets).

The cameraman and the sound recordist did very nicely out of it too.

'Let's just hope,' one said to the other, 'that the Skints won't have to put up with masses of people coming to Woebegone Farm to have a look at the bird.'

But he needn't have worried. True, there were newspaper reporters who snooped around a number of farms near Galapagos House, but though Farmer Skint did, they could see, have geese, they were very ordinary ones.

One person who saw the film on TV and was puzzled was the postman.

'Funny, you know,' he said to his wife, 'but about a year ago, at Woebegone Farm, the farmer's little daughter told me they had a golden goose and I mentioned it to Sir David Otterbury and I could swear that orchard in the film was Farmer Skint's orchard. But I was there delivering mail only yesterday and his geese are ordinary white ones. I tell you what I've just realized – the whole thing was a con! They painted one of those geese with gold paint! What a spoof! I'd never have believed Otterbury was so deceitful!'

For Farmer Skint, who had once been a poor, unfortunate man, things were going swimmingly. True, when he cleaned out Joy's litter tray, he still nurtured a

dim hope that perhaps her droppings would turn gold again, but they never did, and in time the Skints decided that, though Joy would always be welcome in the farmhouse, it was now time that she had a home of her own and, what's more, a husband.

So with some of the money he'd got from the film, John Skint bought a brand-new wooden shed. Joy obviously thought it was beautiful, but Misery and Sorrow were too old for change and preferred their original hut.

He then bought a handsome young

gander (whom Joy also thought
beautiful), a jolly sort of fellow
they named Merriment. Misery
was none too keen on having
another gander about
the place, but
Merriment
was polite to
him and kept out
of his way, and
the young couple
slept happily in the
smart new shed.

One morning the following spring,
Farmer Skint finished the milking and
then, before feeding his pigs and his
chickens and going for his own breakfast,

he went out into the orchard and opened
the door of the old hut to let out Misery
and Sorrow. Then he went to the new
shed to let out Joy
and Merriment.
Then something
made him look
inside it.

   After he'd had
his breakfast
(bacon and
eggs, a

good lining to the stomach), he said to his
wife, 'Guess what, Janet.'

'What?'

'Joy has laid her first egg.'

'Oh, that's wonderful!' she cried.

'It is indeed wonderful,' said Farmer
Skint. 'Guess what, Janet.'

'What?'

'It's a golden egg.'

Read on for an extract from

The
SCHOOLMOUSE

by Dick King-Smith

One
In Which Flora
Makes a Start

Flora was a schoolmouse.

Everyone knows that there are housemice and fieldmice and harvest-mice, and everyone knows that mice who live inside churches are called church-mice. So it's easy to guess where Flora lived.

The school was a very old one, nearly a hundred and fifty years old, in fact, and it stood in the middle of some fields.

Forty-two children went to the school (Infants

and Juniors), and about the same number of mice (fathers, mothers and children) lived permanently in its crumbly old walls and ceilings and dark cupboards, and under its worn wooden floorboards.

But of all these schoolmice, only one grew up to become interested in learning the same lessons as the children.

That was Flora.

It was as though Flora was destined to be a very special schoolmouse, for she was born on the first day of the first term of the new school year, in a hole in the wall of the Infant classroom.

Just next to the teacher's desk there was a cupboard, let in to the old whitewashed stone wall, and just above the doors of this cupboard, there was a small space between two of the stones. High up inside the cupboard a hole had been gnawed, so that a schoolmouse could run up inside and make its way into the space between the stones. From here, if it peeped out, it would have a fine view of the classroom,

including a close-up of the top of the teacher's head, a couple of feet below, as she sat at her desk.

On this particular morning, a particular schoolmouse did not peep out at the Infant classroom, for it was much too busy giving birth to ten babies, one of which was the infant Flora.

All that day the mother mouse lay in the hole in the wall and suckled her new pink naked children, until school was ended, and the children had gone home, and the cleaning ladies had tidied up, and the caretaker had locked up, and the old school was empty of all life save for the jackdaws nesting in the chimneys – and the schoolmice.

Then, at last, easing herself off her sleeping babies, the mother scuttled down into the cupboard and out between its rickety old doors that never quite shut. One jump landed her on top of the teacher's desk, and another on to her chair, down the leg of which she clambered.

In the middle of the classroom floor, she could see, was another mouse, pottering about, whiskers twitching. He was searching for any little bits of anything eatable that the children might have dropped and the cleaning ladies missed.

What a husband, thought the mother mouse, whose name was Hyacinth. Here am I, brought to bed of ten children, and he's not even been to visit me, and sharply she called out, 'Robin!'

Hyacinth's husband was an untidy fellow, whose coat always looked badly in need of grooming. He had lost a part of one ear in a fight and the end of his tail in a trap, and the other schoolmice called him 'Ragged Robin'.

Now, at Hyacinth's summons, he came hurrying towards her.

'Hyce!' he cried (for it was his habit always to address his wife thus – to rhyme with 'mice'). 'Hyce, my love! I haven't seen you all day!'

'No,' said Hyacinth shortly.

'And you seem to have grown thinner, more slender, that is,' said Robin.

'Yes,' said Hyacinth.

'Have you been on a diet?'

'No,' said Hyacinth. 'I have simply lost weight.'

'How?' said Robin.

'You had better come and see.'

Up the leg of the teacher's chair they went and on to the desk-top and up inside the cupboard to the hole in the wall.

'There!' said Hyacinth, and she could not keep a note of pride from her voice. 'All yours!'

'All mine?' said Ragged Robin, and he could not keep a note of anxiety from his voice. Did she expect him to look after this swarm of ugly little pink hairless monsters? He had never had children before. What did fathers do?

'What do I do, Hyce?' he asked nervously.

'Do?' said Hyacinth. 'You don't do anything. It is I who have to suckle them and keep them warm and keep them clean and bring them up to be good mousekins. All you need to do is admire our ten children. Are they not beautiful?'

'Without doubt,' said Robin doubtfully. 'Ten, did you say?'

'Yes, as like as peas in a pod.'

But here, though she was not to know it for quite a while, Hyacinth was wrong. Alike in looks and size the babies might be, and no one, watching them as their hair grew and their eyes opened and they began to crawl about the nest, could possibly have told one from another. Yet among them, as the weeks of term went by and they grew into active, nimble mousekins, was one, a female, who was to develop into the world's most educated schoolmouse.

That one, of course, was Flora.

Whether, in fact, Flora was more intelligent than her nine brothers and sisters, we shall never know. What is certain is that she was more inquisitive. From an early age, Flora liked to poke her nose into everything. Everything interested her, and 'why' was her favourite word. Why did they live in a school? Why was the school sometimes full of people, mostly small, and why, sometimes, empty? Why did all these small people, and some big ones, come to the school? Why did the little ones look at lots of pieces of paper all joined together, with pictures on them and strange black marks and squiggles on the white paper? Why did they hold what looked like thin pieces of wood in their fat little hands and make other black marks on other sheets of paper?

All these things Flora observed, for she alone looked outward from the hole in the wall above the teacher's desk, in the Infant classroom. Always during the school day Hyacinth and the other nine kept well back inside, out of sight, but

Flora crouched at the dark mouth of the hole, watching everything that went on with the greatest curiosity.

Whether she inherited this thirst for knowledge from her matter-of-fact mother or her somewhat scatterbrained father, we shall again never know, but it did not take her long to discover that neither of them knew the answers to all her many 'whys'. It was up to her to find out.

She began the very next morning.

One thing that Flora already knew was that at some time in each day, each child would bring with it one of those joined-together wads of paper, put it down on the desk, and open it. Then the teacher would point at the black marks on the paper, one after another, from left to right, and the child would make different noises.

Day after day, Flora peered down intently, longing to make sense of whatever was going on. But her eyes, though clearly seeing the shape of the printed words on the pages of the books, could not interpret them. And her ears, though clearly hearing the child as it read, could not understand the sounds it made.

Then at last one morning came the great breakthrough that was to make all the difference to Flora's future.

She was watching attentively as usual while a little girl stood beside the teacher with her book. She was a very little girl, just beginning to learn to read, and the book was a very simple one. On each page was a large coloured picture, and below the picture a single word.

The first picture, for example, was of a round red fruit, and below it was written

Flora had never seen an apple, so the sound the child made meant nothing to her, nor had she yet in her short life set eyes on a loaf of

B r e a d

or (mercifully) a

C a t

or on any of the other objects shown as the pages turned. Until the child reached M.

There was a picture that Flora immediately recognized, and below it were five little black marks on the paper, five marks like these —

'Well?' said the teacher.

' "Mouse",' said the child, and in Flora's tiny brain something clicked. Once again she stared hungrily at those five little black marks.

'Mouse,' she said to herself.

Flora had begun to read.

Two

In Which Flora
Reads a Story

The five letters, each so different from its fellows, that made up that first word were the key to Flora's progress.

As she crouched in the hole in the wall, eagerly watching the children reading from their various books, she began to recognize those strangely shaped black marks. This was especially so when one of them was the first letter of a word that meant something to her.

The shape M, for example, stood not only for

'mouse' but for 'mother'. O was for 'owl', and though Flora had never seen one, Hyacinth had told them all what made that melancholy night-time cry outside the old school. And U began a number of common words like 'us' and 'up' and 'under', while S was for lots of things mice did, like 'squeak' and 'scurry' and 'sniff', and E for another, most important one, 'eat'.

One word led to another, and since Flora not only looked but also listened as each of the infants read to the teacher every day, she began to match the shape of the word on the page to the sound that came out of the child's mouth.

Never was there such an attentive, hard-working schoolmouse as Flora.

As Christmas approached at the end of that first term of Flora's life, something else happened which was to further her education.

One weekend, a time when the schoolmice had the place to themselves, Hyacinth called a family conference in the cupboard in the Infant classroom. Ragged Robin had taken little notice of his ten children, being too busy, like all his fellows, searching for food. But now, summoned by his wife, he gave the mousekins his full attention.

'I say, Hyce!' he cried. 'I must congratulate you, my love. You have reared ten splendid children. How strong and healthy they look.'

'They are,' said Hyacinth. 'Say hello to Daddy, children.'

'Hello, Daddy!' chorused the mousekins, all except Flora, who said, 'Hello, Father,' a word that she had recently learned.

'And now,' said Hyacinth, 'say goodbye.'

'To Daddy?' said one of the children.

'To both of us,' said Hyacinth. 'It is time you all went to seek your fortunes out in the great wide school.'

'Yippee!' cried nine of the mousekins, and away they went, out of the cupboard, on to the desk, on to the floor, and out through one or other of the doors of the Infant classroom,

rejoicing that they were infants no longer.

Only Flora remained. She did not at all wish her education to be interrupted.

'Mother,' she said. 'Please can I stay here? I like it here. I wouldn't be in your way.'

'You won't,' said Hyacinth, 'because I'm not stopping. That hole in the wall is draughty. I'm off to find somewhere cosier for the next lot.'

'Next lot, Hyce?' said Robin. 'Next lot of what?'

'Babies, you booby,' said Hyacinth crossly. 'Hadn't you noticed?'

Ragged Robin looked at his wife.

'You seem to have put on weight, grown plumper, that is,' he said. 'I had not realized.'

'Hadn't you?' said Hyacinth.

'Another lot of babies,' said Robin thoughtfully. 'And so soon. I don't know how you do it, Hyce.'

Hyacinth looked at her scruffy husband with

an expression that was a mixture of scorn and resignation.

'Run along, Robin, do,' she said, 'and see if you can find somewhere really comfortable for me. Preferably not in one of the Junior classrooms – children are so noisy.'

'Right ho, Hyce,' said Ragged Robin. 'I'll try the staffroom first. Meet me there,' and off he went.

'Now, young lady,' said Hyacinth, 'just what is this all about? You saw how anxious your brothers and sisters were to be gone. Why do you want to stay here?'

'Please, Mother,' said Flora, 'it's a good place for my lessons.'

'Lessons?'

'Yes, Mother. I'm learning to read.'

'To read?' said Hyacinth. 'What on earth does that mean?'

'To make sense of the words in books, Mother. It's what the schoolchildren are taught to do. They are learning to read and so am I. It's very interesting. At first I could only read the odd word here and there, but before long I hope to be able to read a whole story.'

'Flora!' said Hyacinth sternly. 'I haven't the foggiest idea what you're talking about except that it's rubbish. Whoever heard of mice doing the same things that people do. Next thing, you'll be walking about on your hind legs. You listen to me, my girl – just forget all this non-sense. You've got too high an opinion of yourself, that's your trouble. Giving yourself airs and making out you're cleverer than the rest of us. You're just an ordinary schoolmouse and don't you forget it,' and with this Hyacinth went out through the cupboard doors and dropped carefully down to the desk and on to the floor and away.

Flora climbed up to the hole in the wall and looked out at the Infant classroom. Empty as it was, of humans and mice, there was no one to hear her say, 'I am not an ordinary schoolmouse. I'm sure I'm not. I'm sure I can learn all sorts of things that no mouse has ever learned before, if only I study hard enough, and then I shall be an extraordinary schoolmouse.'

The next day dawned. Flora never forgot that first Monday morning all on her own in the Infant classroom. Not that the other mousekins had interrupted her studies — they and their mother had mostly slept during school hours — but it was lovely to feel she had the place to herself now, ready for another happy week's work.

As if to celebrate her independence, she did something she had never before dared to do.

At midday the bell rang for lunch, and the infants lined up and then left the classroom, followed by the teacher. On her desk, by chance, a reading book had been left wide open, and Flora, seeing this, slipped down and stood before it, her little forepaws upon the edge of the page.

How big and bright the pictures were, now that she was so close, how bold and black the words!

By great good luck the book, called *Billy's Pet*, was open at page one, and when Flora had read that and page two opposite, she very much wanted to know what happened next. But, of course, there was no one to turn over the pages.

Billy, the boy in the story, wanted a pet of his own. 'But is Billy old enough,' his father asked his mother, 'to look after a pet properly?'

Is he, thought Flora? Will they let him have one? And if they do, what will it be? A rabbit? A gerbil? A guinea-pig? What colour will it be? What will it be called?

I must know, thought Flora, and carefully she poked her nose under page two and flipped it over. Once she had the knack of page-turning, keeping each flat with a foot as she read, it was easy. By the time the children came in from the playground at the end of the lunch hour, Flora was safely back in the hole in the wall. On the desk *Billy's Pet* lay open, at the last two pages now.

Flora looked down contentedly.

I must confess, she said to herself, I do like a happy ending.